Words of Wisdom
- Encouraging Bible Verses for Hard Times -

While every precaution has been taken in the preparation of this book, the publisher assumes no responsibility for errors or omissions, or for damages resulting from the use of the information contained herein.

WORDS OF WISDOM: ENCOURAGING BIBLE VERSES FOR HARD TIMES

First edition. April 23, 2023.

Table of Contents

Dedicated to the whole Humanity.
Collected by the greatest AI known to the present day.
Handpicked by a lovely human, Leinad Menelec, Ph.D.

Preface

In times of hardship, it can be difficult to find hope and stay positive. That's why I am excited to share with you "The Promise of Hope: Encouraging Bible Verses for Hard Times." This book is a collection of some of the most powerful and inspiring verses from the Bible that will uplift your spirits, strengthen your faith, and remind you that there is always hope.

As you turn the pages of this book, you will discover verses that will speak directly to your heart and give you the courage to face any challenge. Whether you are going through a difficult time in your personal life, struggling with your faith, or simply in need of some words of wisdom, "The Promise of Hope" has something for you.

These verses have been selected for their ability to offer comfort, guidance, and inspiration in even the darkest of moments. They are a testament to the enduring power of the Bible, and the unwavering love of God. Each one is a reminder that no matter how tough things may seem, there is always a way forward.

I hope that this book will serve as a source of strength and encouragement for you, and that it will remind you of the boundless hope that is available to us all. May the words within its pages bring light to your darkest days, and may they fill your heart with peace and joy.

2 Timothy 1:7

"For God gave us a spirit not of fear but of power and love and self-control."
- 2 Timothy 1:7

This verse reminds us that fear does not come from God, but rather, He has given us the power, love, and self-control to face our fears with confidence.

Philippians 4:13

"I can do all things through Christ who strengthens me."
- Philippians 4:13

This verse encourages us to have faith in Christ, knowing that we can accomplish anything with His strength.

Proverbs 3:5

"Trust in the Lord with all your heart, and do not lean on your own understanding."
- Proverbs 3:5

This verse teaches us to trust in God, even when we cannot comprehend His ways.

Psalm 28:7

"The Lord is my strength and my shield; in him my heart trusts, and I am helped."
- Psalm 28:7

This verse reminds us that God is our protector and that we can trust Him to help us in times of trouble.

Romans 8:28

"And we know that for those who love God all things work together for good, for those who are called according to his purpose."
- Romans 8:28

This verse assures us that God has a plan for our lives, and that He will use all things for our good.

Matthew 6:34

"Therefore do not be anxious about tomorrow, for tomorrow will be anxious for itself. Sufficient for the day is its own trouble."
- Matthew 6:34

This verse reminds us to focus on the present moment and to trust in God's provision for our future.

Proverbs 9:10

"The fear of the Lord is the beginning of wisdom, and the knowledge of the Holy One is insight."
- Proverbs 9:10

This verse encourages us to seek wisdom and understanding by fearing the Lord and gaining knowledge of Him.

Philippians 4:5-6

"Let your reasonableness be known to everyone. The Lord is at hand; do not be anxious about anything, but in everything by prayer and supplication with thanksgiving let your requests be made known to God."
- Philippians 4:5-6

This verse teaches us to bring our concerns to God in prayer, with a heart of thanksgiving, and to trust that He will answer according to His will.

Romans 8:38-39

"For I am sure that neither death nor life, nor angels nor rulers, nor things present nor things to come, nor powers, nor height nor depth, nor anything else in all creation, will be able to separate us from the love of God in Christ Jesus our Lord."
- Romans 8:38-39

This verse reassures us that nothing can separate us from God's love, which is found in Christ Jesus.

Matthew 6:33

"But seek first the kingdom of God and his righteousness, and all these things will be added to you."
- Matthew 6:33

This verse encourages us to prioritize our relationship with God, knowing that He will provide for all our needs.

Psalm 23:1

"The Lord is my shepherd; I shall not want."
- Psalm 23:1

This verse reminds us that God is our provider, protector, and guide, and that we can trust Him to meet all our needs.

Deuteronomy 31:6

"Be strong and courageous. Do not fear or be in dread of them, for it is the Lord your God who goes with you. He will not leave you or forsake you."
- Deuteronomy 31:6

Moses is giving a final address to the Israelites before he dies, encouraging them to be strong and courageous as they prepare to enter the Promised Land. He tells them not to fear or be in dread of their enemies, because the Lord their God will be with them and will never leave them.

Zephaniah 3:17

"The Lord your God is in your midst, a mighty one who will save; he will rejoice over you with gladness; he will quiet you by his love; he will exult over you with loud singing."
- Zephaniah 3:17

This verse speaks of the Lord's love for his people. He is described as a mighty Savior who rejoices over his people with gladness, quiets them with his love, and exults over them with loud singing.

Galatians 6:9

*"And let us not grow weary of doing good, for in due season we will
reap, if we do not give up."*
- Galatians 6:9

Paul is urging the Galatians not to give up in doing good. He encourages them to persevere, because in due time they will reap the rewards if they do not grow weary.

Isaiah 40:31

"But they who wait for the Lord shall renew their strength; they shall mount up with wings like eagles; they shall run and not be weary; they shall walk and not faint."
- Isaiah 40:31

This verse is a promise of renewed strength to those who wait for the Lord. They will soar like eagles, run and not be weary, and walk and not faint.

Romans 12:2

*"Do not be conformed to this world, but be transformed by the renew-
al of your mind, that by testing you may discern what is the will of
God, what is good and acceptable and perfect."*
- Romans 12:2

Paul is urging the Romans to not conform to the patterns of the
world but to be transformed by the renewing of their minds, so that
they may discern what is the will of God.

James 1:12

"Blessed is the man who remains steadfast under trial, for when he has stood the test he will receive the crown of life, which God has promised to those who love him."
- James 1:12

James is speaking about the blessedness of those who remain steadfast under trial, for they will receive the crown of life that God has promised to those who love him.

Psalm 34:18

*"The Lord is near to the brokenhearted and saves the crushed in spir-
it."*
- Psalm 34:18

The psalmist speaks of God's nearness to those who are brokenhearted and crushed in spirit. He is their Savior and delivers them
from their troubles.

Philippians 4:19

"And my God will supply every need of yours according to his riches in glory in Christ Jesus."
- Philippians 4:19

Paul is telling the Philippians that God will supply all their needs according to his riches in glory in Christ Jesus.

Joshua 1:9

"Have I not commanded you? Be strong and courageous. Do not be frightened, and do not be dismayed, for the Lord your God is with you wherever you go."
- Joshua 1:9

God is speaking to Joshua, urging him to be strong and courageous as he prepares to lead the Israelites into the Promised Land. He reminds Joshua that he will always be with him wherever he goes.

Proverbs 2:6

"For the Lord gives wisdom; from his mouth come knowledge and understanding."
- Proverbs 2:6

This verse speaks of the source of wisdom, which comes from the Lord. True knowledge and understanding come from his mouth.

Ephesians 2:8

"For by grace you have been saved through faith. And this is not your own doing; it is the gift of God."
- Ephesians 2:8

Paul is reminding the Ephesians that their salvation is a gift from God, not something they have earned or accomplished on their own.

John 14:1

"Let not your hearts be troubled. Believe in God; believe also in me."
- John 14:1

Jesus is speaking to his disciples, telling them not to let their hearts be troubled, but to believe in God and in him.

2 Corinthians 5:17

"Therefore, if anyone is in Christ, he is a new creation. The old has passed away; behold, the new has come."
- 2 Corinthians 5:17

Paul is telling the Corinthians that if they are in Christ, they are a new creation. The old has passed away, and the new has come.

Galatians 5:22-23

"But the fruit of the Spirit is love, joy, peace, patience, kindness, good-ness, faithfulness, gentleness, self-control; against such things there is no law."
- Galatians 5:22-23

Paul is describing the fruits of the Spirit, which include love, joy, peace, patience, kindness, goodness, faithfulness, gentleness, and self-control.

Galatians 6:7

"Do not be deceived: God is not mocked, for whatever one sows, that will he also reap."
- Galatians 6:7

Paul is warning the Galatians not to be deceived: they will reap what they sow. If they sow to please the flesh, they will reap destruction; but if they sow to please the Spirit, they will reap eternal life.

Psalm 18:2

"The Lord is my rock and my fortress and my deliverer, my God, my rock, in whom I take refuge, my shield, and the horn of my salvation, my stronghold."
- Psalm 18:2

The psalmist describes the Lord as his rock, fortress, deliverer, shield, and stronghold. He takes refuge in him.

Mark 8:36

"For what does it profit a man to gain the whole world and forfeit his soul?"
- Mark 8:36

Jesus is speaking to his disciples, warning them that it is not worth gaining the whole world if it means forfeiting their souls.

John 16:33

"I have said these things to you, that in me you may have peace. In the world you will have tribulation. But take heart; I have overcome the world."
- John 16:33

In this verse, Jesus is comforting his disciples by reminding them that they will face trials and difficulties in the world, but they can find peace in him. He encourages them to be courageous because he has already overcome the world. This verse teaches us that although life can be challenging, we can find peace in Jesus and his victory can inspire us to persevere.

Psalm 46:10

"Be still, and know that I am God. I will be exalted among the nations, I will be exalted in the earth!"
- Psalm 46:10

This verse is a reminder to be still and know that God is in control. It reminds us that no matter what is happening in our lives, God is the one who ultimately reigns over everything. This verse encourages us to trust God and to seek his guidance and wisdom in our lives.

Jeremiah 29:7

"But seek the welfare of the city where I have sent you into exile, and pray to the Lord on its behalf, for in its welfare you will find your welfare."
- Jeremiah 29:7

In this verse, God instructs the Israelites who were in exile in Babylon to seek the welfare of the city where they were living. God reminds them that if they pray for the well-being of the city, they too will benefit. This verse teaches us that we should care for the well-being of our communities and seek to make a positive impact in the world.

1 John 4:7

"Beloved, let us love one another, for love is from God, and whoever loves has been born of God and knows God."
- 1 John 4:7

This verse reminds us that love comes from God and those who love have been born of God and know him. It teaches us that love is a defining characteristic of a true follower of Jesus Christ. We are called to love one another as God has loved us.

Romans 8:18

"For I consider that the sufferings of this present time are not worth comparing with the glory that is to be revealed to us."
- Romans 8:18

This verse encourages us to persevere through the difficulties we may face in life. It reminds us that the present sufferings are temporary and are not worth comparing to the glory that will be revealed to us in the future. This verse teaches us that we should keep our eyes fixed on the eternal hope that we have in Christ.

2 Corinthians 3:18

"And we all, with unveiled face, beholding the glory of the Lord, are being transformed into the same image from one degree of glory to another. For this comes from the Lord who is the Spirit."
- 2 Corinthians 3:18

This verse reminds us that as we behold the glory of the Lord, we are being transformed into his image. It teaches us that the Holy Spirit is at work in us, transforming us from one degree of glory to another. This verse encourages us to continue seeking God's presence in our lives, knowing that he is at work in us, transforming us into his image.

Colossians 3:15

The verse in Colossians 3:15 encourages us to let the peace of Christ rule in our hearts, reminding us that we were called to live in one body and to be thankful. When we allow the peace of Christ to rule in our hearts, it brings a sense of calm and harmony to our lives and relationships.

Philippians 4:7

"And the peace of God, which surpasses all understanding, will guard your hearts and your minds in Christ Jesus."
- Philippians 4:7

In Philippians 4:7, we're reminded that the peace of God surpasses all understanding and that it will guard our hearts and minds in Christ Jesus. This verse reminds us that even in the midst of chaos and turmoil, God's peace is available to us if we trust in Him.

Romans 15:13

"May the God of hope fill you with all joy and peace in believing, so that by the power of the Holy Spirit you may abound in hope."
- Romans 15:13

Romans 15:13 encourages us to abound in hope through the power of the Holy Spirit. When we believe in God's promises and trust in His plan, we can experience the joy and peace that comes from a hopeful heart.

1 Peter 2:9

"But you are a chosen race, a royal priesthood, a holy nation, a people for his own possession, that you may proclaim the excellencies of him who called you out of darkness into his marvelous light."
- 1 Peter 2:9

1 Peter 2:9 reminds us of our identity as a chosen race, a royal priesthood, and a holy nation. We are called to proclaim the excellencies of God who has called us out of darkness and into His marvelous light. This verse reminds us that we are valuable to God and have a unique purpose in His plan.

Matthew 22:37

"And he said to him, "You shall love the Lord your God with all your heart and with all your soul and with all your mind."
- Matthew 22:37

Matthew 22:37 reminds us to love the Lord with all our heart, soul, and mind. This verse encourages us to prioritize our relationship with God above all else, seeking Him first in all aspects of our lives.

1 John 1:9

"If we confess our sins, he is faithful and just to forgive us our sins and to cleanse us from all unrighteousness."
- 1 John 1:9

1 John 1:9 reminds us that when we confess our sins, God is faithful and just to forgive us and cleanse us from all unrighteousness. This verse reminds us of the power of repentance and the gift of forgiveness through Christ.

Hebrews 10:23

*"Let us hold fast the confession of our hope without wavering, for he
who promised is faithful."*
- Hebrews 10:23

Hebrews 10:23 encourages us to hold fast to our confession of
hope without wavering, trusting that God who promised is faithful. This verse reminds us of the importance of perseverance in our
faith and the assurance we have in God's promises.

Philippians 1:21

"For to me to live is Christ, and to die is gain."
- Philippians 1:21

Philippians 1:21 declares that for the Apostle Paul, to live is Christ, and to die is gain. This verse reminds us that our lives are not our own, and we have been called to live for Christ and His purposes.

Proverbs 3:6

"In all your ways acknowledge him, and he will make straight your paths."
- Proverbs 3:6

Proverbs 3:6 reminds us to acknowledge God in all our ways and trust Him to make our paths straight. This verse encourages us to seek God's guidance in all aspects of our lives and trust that He will lead us in the right direction.

Colossians 3:17

"And whatever you do, in word or deed, do everything in the name of the Lord Jesus, giving thanks to God the Father through him."
- Colossians 3:17

Colossians 3:17 reminds us that whatever we do, in word or deed, we should do it in the name of the Lord Jesus, giving thanks to God the Father through Him. This verse encourages us to live our lives with intention and purpose, always seeking to honor God in everything we do.

John 3:16

"For God so loved the world, that he gave his only Son, that whoever believes in him should not perish but have eternal life."
- John 3:16

John 3:16 is perhaps the most famous verse in the Bible, reminding us of God's great love for us, demonstrated through the sacrifice of His Son, Jesus. This verse is a beautiful reminder of the gift of salvation and the hope we have in Christ.

2 Corinthians 12:9

"But he said to me, "My grace is sufficient for you, for my power is made perfect in weakness." Therefore I will boast all the more gladly of my weaknesses, so that the power of Christ may rest upon me."
- 2 Corinthians 12:9

2 Corinthians 12:9 reminds us that God's grace is sufficient for us, and His power is made perfect in our weakness. This verse reminds us that we don't have to have it all together or be perfect for God to use us, but rather it is in our weakness that God's strength can shine through.

Philippians 4:13

"I can do all things through him who strengthens me."
- Philippians 4:13

Philippians 4:13 declares that we can do all things through Christ who strengthens us. This verse reminds us that we don't have to rely on our own strength or abilities, but rather we can trust in God's strength to empower us to do what He has called us to do.

Romans 6:23

"For the wages of sin is death, but the free gift of God is eternal life in Christ Jesus our Lord."
- Romans 6:23

This verse speaks to the reality of sin and the consequences that come with it. But there's good news - God offers us a free gift of eternal life through Jesus. This gift is available to all who believe and trust in Jesus as their Lord and Savior. Through Him, we can have hope for a new life, free from the power of sin and death.

2 Peter 1:19

"And we have something more sure, the prophetic word, to which you will do well to pay attention as to a lamp shining in a dark place, until the day dawns and the morning star rises in your hearts."
- 2 Peter 1:19

This verse reminds us of the importance of paying attention to the prophetic word, which is the Word of God. It serves as a lamp that guides us through the darkness of life, leading us towards the hope of a new day. The morning star represents Jesus, who shines His light on us and helps us see the way forward.

Hebrews 4:12

"For the word of God is living and active, sharper than any two-edged sword, piercing to the division of soul and of spirit, of joints and of marrow, and discerning the thoughts and intentions of the heart."
- Hebrews 4:12

This verse speaks to the power of God's Word, which is able to cut through to the very depths of our being. It exposes our true thoughts and intentions, and helps us see ourselves as we truly are. But it also offers us hope and healing, as we turn to God and allow His Word to transform us from the inside out.

1 Peter 1:3

"Blessed be the God and Father of our Lord Jesus Christ! According to his great mercy, he has caused us to be born again to a living hope through the resurrection of Jesus Christ from the dead."
- 1 Peter 1:3

This verse reminds us of the incredible mercy of God, who offers us a new life through Jesus. We can be born again, transformed from the inside out, and filled with a living hope that never fades. This hope comes through the resurrection of Jesus, who conquered death and offers us new life in Him.

Galatians 2:20

"I have been crucified with Christ. It is no longer I who live, but Christ who lives in me. And the life I now live in the flesh I live by faith in the Son of God, who loved me and gave himself for me."
- Galatians 2:20

This verse speaks to the transformation that takes place when we give our lives to Jesus. We die to ourselves and are reborn in Him, as Christ lives in us and through us. Our old ways of living are replaced with a new way of life, based on faith in Jesus and His love for us.

Psalm 100:5

"For the Lord is good; his steadfast love endures forever, and his faithfulness to all generations."
- Psalm 100:5

This verse reminds us of the goodness of God, and His never-ending love and faithfulness. We can trust in Him and His promises, knowing that He will never let us down or abandon us. His love endures through all generations, and we can rely on Him to guide us through life's ups and downs.

2 Corinthians 5:14-15

"For the love of Christ controls us, because we have concluded this: that one has died for all, therefore all have died; and he died for all, that those who live might no longer live for themselves but for him who for their sake died and was raised."
- 2 Corinthians 5:14-15

The love of Christ is a powerful force that controls us and directs our actions. We know that Jesus died for all, so that we might die to our selfish desires and live for Him who died and was raised for us. As we allow the love of Christ to rule our hearts, we are compelled to love and serve others, just as He did.

Psalm 28:7

"The Lord is my strength and my shield; in him my heart trusts, and I am helped; my heart exults, and with my song I give thanks to him."
- Psalm 28:7

When we trust in the Lord, we find strength and protection. He is our shield and our helper in times of need. Our hearts can rejoice and be filled with gratitude as we sing praises to Him who has been faithful to us.

Hebrews 12:1

*"Therefore, since we are surrounded by so great a cloud of witnesses,
let us also lay aside every weight, and sin which clings so closely, and
let us run with endurance the race that is set before us."*
- Hebrews 12:1

We are not alone in our faith journey. We are surrounded by a great
cloud of witnesses who have gone before us and have lived out their
faith with perseverance. As we run the race set before us, we must
lay aside any hindrances or sins that would weigh us down. With
endurance and a steadfast focus on Jesus, we can finish the race
well.

Matthew 5:6

Those who hunger and thirst for righteousness are blessed because they will be satisfied. When we seek after God and His righteousness, we are filled with His love, joy, and peace. Our souls find rest and satisfaction in Him.

Hebrews 4:15

"For we do not have a high priest who is unable to sympathize with our weaknesses, but one who in every respect has been tempted as we are, yet without sin."
- Hebrews 4:15

We have a High Priest, Jesus Christ, who can sympathize with our weaknesses because He has experienced every temptation and struggle that we face. He is able to help us in our time of need because He understands us completely.

Matthew 4:4

"But he answered, "It is written, "'Man shall not live by bread alone, but by every word that comes from the mouth of God.'"
- Matthew 4:4

Our physical sustenance is not enough to satisfy our deepest needs. We must also feed on the Word of God, which gives us spiritual nourishment and sustains our souls. When we abide in His Word, we are filled with His truth, wisdom, and guidance.

Isaiah 55:9

"For as the heavens are higher than the earth, so are my ways higher than your ways and my thoughts than your thoughts."
- Isaiah 55:9

This verse reminds us that God's ways and thoughts are beyond our comprehension. It can be easy to get caught up in our limited understanding of situations, but we must trust that God has a greater plan and purpose for everything. We can find comfort in knowing that God sees the bigger picture and is always working things out for our good, even when we don't understand.

Psalm 68:19

"Blessed be the Lord, who daily bears us up; God is our salvation."
- Psalm 68:19

This verse is a beautiful reminder that God is always with us, bearing our burdens and providing us with the strength we need to overcome any obstacle. We can trust in Him as our salvation, knowing that He has already won the victory for us through His death and resurrection. We can find peace in knowing that we are never alone and that God is always working for our good.

1 Thessalonians 5:11

"Therefore encourage one another and build one another up, just as you are doing."
- 1 Thessalonians 5:11

This verse reminds us of the importance of building each other up in love and encouragement. We are all part of one body in Christ, and it is our responsibility to support and uplift one another as we journey through life. By sharing words of kindness and encouragement, we can help each other grow stronger in our faith and draw closer to God.

Matthew 5:16

"In the same way, let your light shine before others, so that they may see your good works and give glory to your Father who is in heaven."
- Matthew 5:16

This verse encourages us to be a light in the world, shining the love and goodness of God through our actions and words. By living a life of kindness, compassion, and service, we can inspire others to seek after God and give glory to Him. We are called to be ambassadors of Christ in the world, sharing His love with all those we encounter.

Matthew 21:22

"And whatever you ask in prayer, you will receive, if you have faith."
- Matthew 21:22

This verse reminds us of the power of prayer and the importance of having faith. When we approach God with faith and trust in His goodness, we can be confident that He will answer our prayers according to His will. This doesn't mean that we will always get what we want, but it does mean that God will give us what is best for us in His perfect timing.

Galatians 5:16

This verse encourages us to live our lives guided by the Holy Spirit rather than our own desires. When we submit ourselves to the leading of the Spirit, we can overcome the temptations of the flesh and live a life that honors God. By walking in the Spirit, we can experience the peace, joy, and fulfillment that come from living in close relationship with God.

Romans 12:2

This verse reminds us that we are not meant to conform to the ways of this world, but rather we are called to transform our minds and hearts through the renewal that comes from God. When we renew our minds, we are able to see God's will more clearly and discern what is good and acceptable in his sight. It is through this transformation that we can live our lives in a way that pleases God.

Psalm 145:18

"The Lord is near to all who call on him, to all who call on him in truth."
- Psalm 145:18

This verse is a comforting reminder that the Lord is always near to us and ready to listen to our prayers when we call upon him in truth. Whether we are feeling lost or alone, we can always turn to God and find comfort in his presence.

James 4:6

"But he gives more grace. Therefore it says, "God opposes the proud but gives grace to the humble."
- James 4:6

This verse reminds us that God's grace is available to all who are humble and willing to receive it. It is only when we recognize our need for God's grace and acknowledge our own weaknesses that we can fully experience the richness of his love and mercy.

Ephesians 2:8-9

"For by grace you have been saved through faith. And this is not your own doing; it is the gift of God, not a result of works, so that no one may boast."
- Ephesians 2:8-9

This verse is a powerful reminder that our salvation is not something we can earn through our own efforts or good deeds. Rather, it is a gift of God's grace that we receive through faith in Jesus Christ. This gift is freely given, so that no one can boast about their own righteousness, but instead we can humbly receive it with gratitude and praise.

Hebrews 11:6

"And without faith it is impossible to please him, for whoever would draw near to God must believe that he exists and that he rewards those who seek him."
- Hebrews 11:6

This verse emphasizes the importance of faith in our relationship with God. It is through faith that we are able to please God and draw near to him. We must believe that he exists and that he rewards those who seek him, trusting that he is faithful to his promises.

1 Thessalonians 5:16-18

"Rejoice always, pray without ceasing, give thanks in all circum-stances; for this is the will of God in Christ Jesus for you."
- 1 Thessalonians 5:16-18

This verse reminds us that as believers, we are called to a life of joy, prayer, and gratitude. We should always rejoice in the Lord, praying without ceasing and giving thanks in all circumstances. This is the will of God for our lives, as we seek to grow closer to him and reflect his love to the world.

Colossians 4:6

"Let your speech always be gracious, seasoned with salt, so that you may know how you ought to answer each person."
- Colossians 4:6

As followers of Christ, we are called to be gracious in our speech and interactions with others. Our words should be seasoned with salt, meaning they should be both truthful and uplifting, bringing out the best in others. By doing so, we can better discern how to answer each person, treating them with kindness and respect.

Romans 5:1

"Therefore, since we have been justified by faith, we have peace with God through our Lord Jesus Christ."
- Romans 5:1

Through faith in Jesus Christ, we are made right with God and can have peace with Him. No longer do we need to fear or worry about our standing with God, for we are justified and made righteous by our faith in Him. This peace with God brings us comfort, joy, and hope for the future.

2 Corinthians 4:16

"So we do not lose heart. Though our outer self is wasting away, our inner self is being renewed day by day."
- 2 Corinthians 4:16

As we go through life, our bodies may age and weaken, but our inner selves, our spirits, can be renewed each day by the Holy Spirit. We do not lose heart in the face of trials and difficulties, for we have a hope that sustains us and empowers us to endure.

Psalm 23:1-3

"The Lord is my shepherd; I shall not want. He makes me lie down in green pastures. He leads me beside still waters. He restores my soul. He leads me in paths of righteousness for his name's sake."
- Psalm 23:1-3

God, our Shepherd, leads us to rest in green pastures and to drink from still waters. He restores our souls and guides us along the paths of righteousness, all for His glory. With the Lord as our Shepherd, we lack nothing and can trust in His provision and care.

Revelation 21:5

"And he who was seated on the throne said, "Behold, I am making all things new." Also he said, "Write this down, for these words are trust-
worthy and true.""
- Revelation 21:5

God is the author of new beginnings, and in Christ, He is making all things new. His promise to renew and restore all things is trustworthy and true, offering us hope for the future and the assurance that He is making all things right.

James 1:5

When we face decisions or situations that require wisdom, we can turn to God and ask for His guidance. He gives generously to all who ask, without reproach or judgment. With His wisdom, we can navigate life's challenges and make decisions that honor Him.

Hebrews 4:16

"Let us then with confidence draw near to the throne of grace, that we may receive mercy and find grace to help in time of need."
- Hebrews 4:16

As believers in Jesus, we can approach God's throne with confidence, knowing that He welcomes us with mercy and grace. We can bring our needs before Him, knowing that He cares for us and will provide the help we need. With His grace, we can face any situation with courage and hope.

1 John 4:16

"So we have come to know and to believe the love that God has for us. God is love, and whoever abides in love abides in God, and God abides in him."
- 1 John 4:16

1 John 4:16 reminds us that God is love and that whoever abides in love abides in God, and God abides in them. This means that when we love others, we are showing God's love to the world and we are also experiencing God's love in our own lives.

Jeremiah 29:11

"For I know the plans I have for you, declares the Lord, plans for welfare and not for evil, to give you a future and a hope."
- Jeremiah 29:11

Jeremiah 29:11 assures us that God has plans for our lives, plans for our welfare and not for evil, plans to give us a future and a hope. This means that no matter what difficulties we may face in life, we can trust that God has a purpose and a plan for us that will ultimately lead to our good.

Psalm 55:22

"Cast your burden on the Lord, and he will sustain you; he will never permit the righteous to be moved."
- Psalm 55:22

Psalm 55:22 encourages us to cast our burdens on the Lord, knowing that He will sustain us and never allow the righteous to be moved. This means that we can bring all of our worries, fears, and concerns to God in prayer, trusting that He will provide the strength and support we need to persevere through any challenges.

Lamentations 3:25

"The Lord is good to those who wait for him, to the soul who seeks him."
- Lamentations 3:25

Lamentations 3:25 reminds us that the Lord is good to those who wait for Him and seek Him. This means that when we patiently and earnestly seek God, we can trust that He will reveal Himself to us in powerful ways and bless us with His goodness and grace.

1 Thessalonians 5:14

1 Thessalonians 5:14 urges us to encourage and support one another in our journey of faith, admonishing the idle, encouraging the faint-hearted, helping the weak, and being patient with them all. This means that we are called to be a community of love and support, using our gifts and talents to help one another grow and thrive in our relationship with God.

Hebrews 10:24-25

"And let us consider how to stir up one another to love and good works, not neglecting to meet together, as is the habit of some, but encouraging one another, and all the more as you see the Day drawing near."
- Hebrews 10:24-25

Hebrews 10:24-25 encourages us to consider how we can stir up one another to love and good works, not neglecting to meet together, but encouraging one another even more as we see the day of Christ's return drawing near. This means that we should prioritize gathering with other believers and using our time together to build each other up and spur each other on in our pursuit of God.

Philippians 4:6

"Do not be anxious about anything, but in everything by prayer and supplication with thanksgiving let your requests be made known to God."
- Philippians 4:6

Philippians 4:6 advises us not to be anxious about anything, but to bring our requests to God in prayer and supplication with thanksgiving. This means that we can bring all of our worries and concerns to God in prayer, trusting that He will provide for our needs and give us the peace and strength we need to face any challenge.

Romans 8:6

*"For to set the mind on the flesh is death, but to set the mind on the
Spirit is life and peace."*
- Romans 8:6

In Romans 8:6, we are reminded that if we focus on the desires
of our flesh, we will only experience death. However, if we set our
minds on the Spirit, we will experience life and peace. This encourages us to seek a deeper spiritual connection and to prioritize our
spiritual health above our worldly desires.

Philippians 4:8

"Finally, brothers, whatever is true, whatever is honorable, whatever is just, whatever is pure, whatever is lovely, whatever is commendable, if there is any excellence, if there is anything worthy of praise, think about these things."
- Philippians 4:8

Philippians 4:8 tells us to focus our thoughts on things that are true, honorable, just, pure, lovely, commendable, excellent, and praiseworthy. By focusing on these things, we can fill our minds with positivity and goodness, which can lead to greater happiness and fulfillment.

1 John 5:20

"And we know that the Son of God has come and has given us under-standing, so that we may know him who is true; and we are in him who is true, in his Son Jesus Christ. He is the true God and eternal life."
- 1 John 5:20

1 John 5:20 reminds us that Jesus is the true God who has given us the understanding to know Him. By knowing and following Him, we can experience eternal life.

Romans 3:23

"For all have sinned and fall short of the glory of God."
- Romans 3:23

Romans 3:23 acknowledges that all have sinned and fallen short of the glory of God. This verse reminds us that we are not perfect and that we all make mistakes. However, it also offers hope by highlighting our need for God's grace and forgiveness.

Colossians 3:16

"Let the word of Christ dwell in you richly, teaching and admonishing one another in all wisdom, singing psalms and hymns and spiritual songs, with thankfulness in your hearts to God."
- Colossians 3:16

Colossians 3:16 urges us to let the word of Christ dwell in us richly, teaching and admonishing one another in all wisdom, singing psalms, hymns, and spiritual songs with thankfulness in our hearts to God. This verse reminds us of the importance of immersing ourselves in the Word of God and sharing it with others.

James 1:2-4

"Count it all joy, my brothers, when you meet trials of various kinds, for you know that the testing of your faith produces steadfastness. And let steadfastness have its full effect, that you may be perfect and complete, lacking in nothing."
- James 1:2-4

James 1:2-4 encourages us to count it all joy when we face trials, knowing that the testing of our faith produces steadfastness. This reminds us that even in difficult times, God is working in us to strengthen our faith and prepare us for greater things.

2 Corinthians 12:9

"But he said to me, 'My grace is sufficient for you, for my power is made perfect in weakness.' Therefore I will boast all the more gladly of my weaknesses, so that the power of Christ may rest upon me."
- 2 Corinthians 12:9

2 Corinthians 12:9 reassures us that God's grace is sufficient for us, and that His power is made perfect in our weaknesses. This encourages us to embrace our weaknesses and allow God's strength to work through us.

Proverbs 3:5-6

"Trust in the Lord with all your heart, and do not lean on your own understanding. In all your ways acknowledge him, and he will make straight your paths."
- Proverbs 3:5-6

Proverbs 3:5-6 reminds us to trust in the Lord with all our hearts and not to lean on our own understanding. This encourages us to rely on God's guidance and wisdom in all areas of our lives.

Philippians 2:3-4

"Do nothing from rivalry or conceit, but in humility count others more significant than yourselves. Let each of you look not only to his own interests, but also to the interests of others."
- Philippians 2:3-4

Philippians 2:3-4 urges us to practice humility, counting others more significant than ourselves, and looking not only to our own interests but also to the interests of others. This verse reminds us of the importance of putting others before ourselves and loving our neighbors as ourselves.

Proverbs 18:22

"He who finds a wife finds a good thing and obtains favor from the Lord."
- Proverbs 18:22

Proverbs 18:22 reminds us that finding a spouse is a blessing from the Lord. This verse encourages us to value and honor the institution of marriage.

Romans 12:9-10

"Let love be genuine. Abhor what is evil; hold fast to what is good. Love one another with brotherly affection. Outdo one another in showing honor."
- Romans 12:9-10

Romans 12:9-10 urges us to let our love be genuine, to abhor what is evil, to hold fast to what is good, and to love one another with brotherly affection, outdoing one another in showing honor. This verse reminds us of the importance of living a life that reflects the love of Christ and treating others with respect and kindness.

Colossians 3:14

"And above all these put on love, which binds everything together in perfect harmony."
- Colossians 3:14

Colossians 3:14 encourages us to put on love, which binds everything together in perfect harmony. This verse reminds us that love is the most important thing we can possess and share with others.

Numbers 6:24-26

*"The Lord bless you and keep you; the Lord make his face to shine up-
on you and be gracious to you; the Lord lift up his countenance upon
you and give you peace."*
- Numbers 6:24-26

Numbers 6:24-26 offers a beautiful blessing that reminds us of
God's love, grace, and peace. This verse encourages us to seek God's
blessings and to trust in His goodness.

2 Thessalonians 3:3

"But the Lord is faithful. He will establish you and guard you against the evil one."
- 2 Thessalonians 3:3

2 Thessalonians 3:3 reassures us that the Lord is faithful and will establish us and guard us against the evil one. This verse reminds us of God's faithfulness and encourages us to trust in Him, even in difficult times.

Acknowledgements

I want to begin by expressing my deepest gratitude to the Almighty God, who is the source of all hope and inspiration. Without His divine grace and guidance, this book would not have been possible. To all the readers of "The Promise of Hope", I want to thank you for your interest in this book, and I pray that the words within its pages will uplift and inspire you.

I would like to extend my heartfelt thanks to the team at OpenAI, making ChatGPT publicly available, it has been instrumental in shaping this book and bringing it to fruition.

I would also like to thank my family and friends for their unwavering support and encouragement. Your love and faith in me have been a constant source of strength, and I am blessed to have you in my life.

Finally, I would like to dedicate this book to anyone who is going through a difficult time, and who needs a message of hope and inspiration. May the verses within these pages remind you that you are not alone, and that there is always a glimmer of hope, even in the darkest of times.

Thank you all, and God bless.

Don't miss out!

Visit the website below and you can sign up to receive emails whenever Leinad Menelec, Ph.D. publishes a new book. There's no charge and no obligation.

https://books2read.com/r/B-A-MERW-LNUHC

BOOKS 2 READ

Connecting independent readers to independent writers.

Also by Leinad Menelec, Ph.D.

Words of Wisdom

Words of Wisdom: Powerful Quotes to Inspire and Bring Positive Change to Your Life

Words of Wisdom: Encouraging Bible Verses for Hard Times

Standalone

The Big Questions of Life: A Conversation with ChatGPT